I0571249

THE ZOMBIES

by
D MARSTON

UPWARDS

CUSTOM
PRESS

Portland OR
—2017—

Printed in the United States of America

Edited by: D Marston
Cover art by D Marston and Cyrus Wraith Walker
Interior design & cover layout by Cyrus Wraith Walker. cyrusfiction@gmail.com

Illustrations by D Marston

Published by
Upwards Custom Press
3504 N.E. 109th
Portland, OR. 97220
United States of America
Contact: upwardscustompress@gmail.com

First Trade Paperback
ISBN-13: 978-0692875858

CONTENTS

INTRODUCTION

The compositions that follow were written as a bridge to bring me back to what might be construed as the real world. In a time when what was real had deconstructed into looser and ever looser terms. For that the dead should walk the earth can only be a grim madness, where anything certain is lost to the fire. If it were not terror enough that we should be subject as witnesses to decay and blight crawling from their sepulchers, if, by itself, that the animate dead should pollute the fair sanity of our lives was not sufficient, but that the cruelty of this unnatural state should overflow with grief and hysteria. For the ghost-less antagonists were, to our great fear, not just the contents of tombs spilled forth in our midst, but were vile of a sort that was beyond our common reason. For the aberration of this madness rolled as a mob of slayers! Their mouth as death calling from the grave. Seeking to spoil the hot blood of the living. And so our reality had been parted at the seams. In shock and disbelief, the color draining from our faces.

Poetry, I had found, was the only retelling I could manage. For what can be told of these things when what they are is beyond understanding? These unnatural and bane events have no context, no place in the world. And yet here it is. As a gross and terrific dream that is made worse in that awaking offers no release. For the raw and penetrating scourge had reached with morose fingers to spike our blood with fears gross darkness. To gather my thoughts onto these pages was with strained and tense effort, only poetries raw pallet would, for me, serve this purpose. Making it possible that I might sift through the wreckage to salvage from the madness what it is that I have seen. And to fathom from it a response.

In this way I found myself returning. Slowly, as it would be, like walking through waist deep water. Returning to solid ground. Not the ground of the life that once was. But the ground of existence beyond terror, beyond fear. For which if we contend not, then the boorish villains would too soon on our heals fall like lions. And of a certainty, there would be none to deliver, when all men have fled.

For the world we knew folded in on itself. And in turn unpackaged the contents of our miseries. The broken segments of poems were, for me, a reflection of a fragmented world. For I also had been broken, damaged and strewn into pieces. So from me must come the fragmented, the partial, the particular remnants. And yet I wonder, for the weight, the force of what might be reported, what more could be said than what is fused and pressed into the sketches of these arranged words.

The act of rendering with pen and paper these reflections became for me a means to cross over from that cloud of unknowing. To restore some compass to the obscurity of my thoughts. The following is not a history of what happened. I am not reporting the facts of events as they transpired. For such a reasonable thing was beyond me. There are no facts here. No explanation. As there are no facts of a car wreck as it is happening. It is only violence. Sure and determinate, unsympathetic. We can only see it coming. This is what it is like. This is what I have seen. In slow motion. As the days shattered as a windshield. As the months heaved into the air as passengers lifted from their seats. And the noise and the clamor and the injury. Our next memory is of bodies littering the interstate. And the smell of gasoline and of smoke.

Though it would seem that to death belongs the preeminence. And everything that could break, in fact had. But in the passing of time, it seems to me that the roar of our losses is material. And the dominion of death is as well of the same. So it seems to me that there must be more to being human than this carnal vainer. And so, as it must be, meaning and importance, if you believe in such things, are couched in the immaterial. Life, as it were, I have come to believe, belongs to such as these.

—D Marston

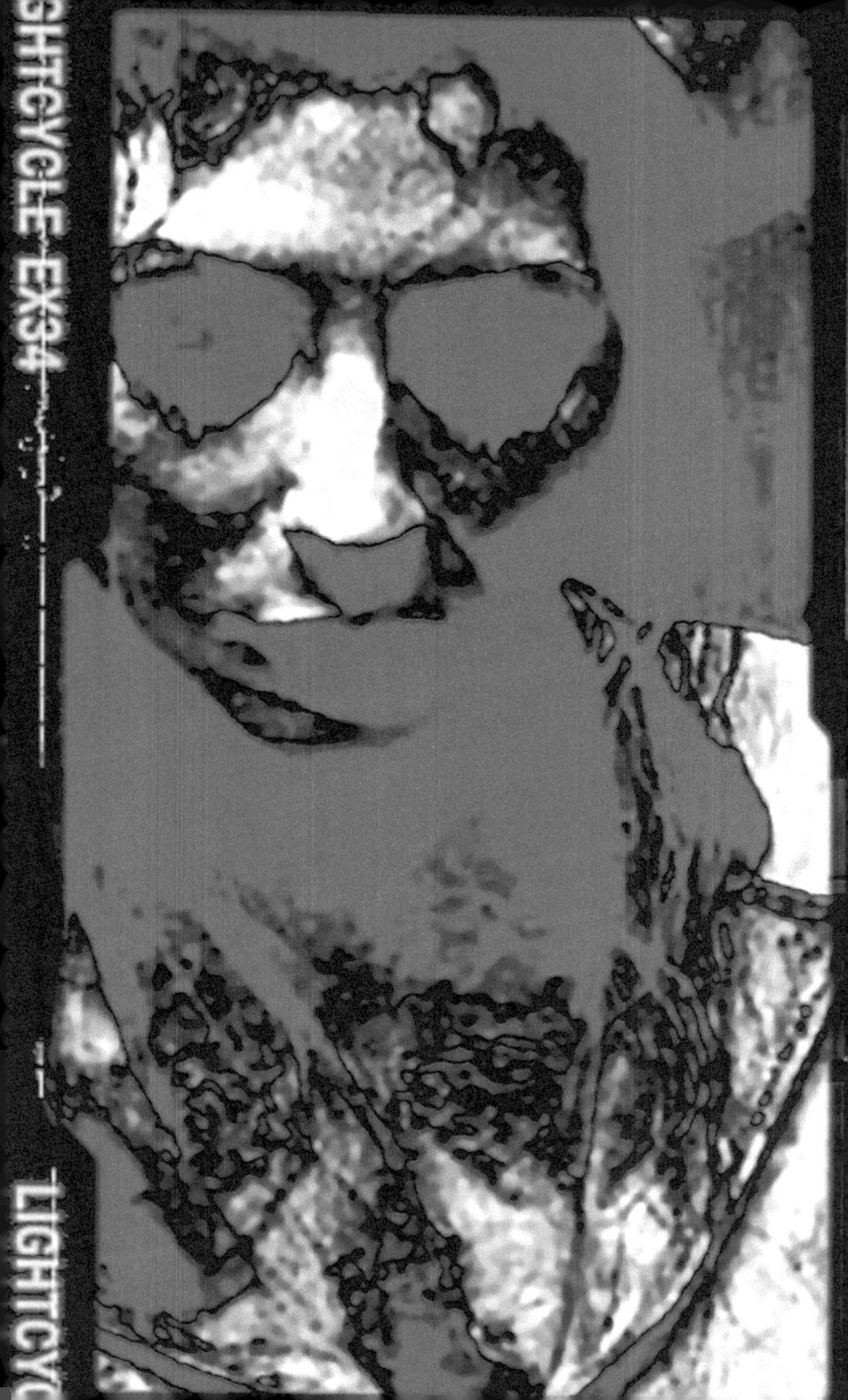

PART 1
WHAT CAN CHANGE IN A DAY

DAY ZERO

no one would have believed
nor could have one known
for as we had busied our selves
with the cares and the concerns
for on these things
does not the world turn?
for the commonness of our affairs
and the progress of our prodigious flight

when once our roof tops touched the clouds
and our satellites we hung
even in further heights
for the world for us was turning
and benefit we would glean
at every course and causeway

so our substance we thought
was as iron as is iron to wood immovable
for we had dug down to set our stones
and we had overturned the hills in the same
and so we are chrome
and we are towers
because we have made it so
and in this way and for this reason
we could not have imagined
whence comes our undoing

surprising thus was the repot
for in no less than the stretch of an hour
did our place in the world tare as fabric
and our walls fell in a day

though we fled the city
only to abandon our cars
on the grid locked interstate
it became all to clear
even at the beginning
that there was no where to run

so here the sun would set
and here the night would find us
and the great stature of our pride
and of our vast achievements
had become as though
a thing that knew us not

so our gainful world turned its back

we have become as summer fruit
but autumn has come and autumn has gone
for in winter is forgotten
what in summer once was
so the branch is stricken bare
so the dead walk amongst the living
so our fortunes also
have fallen with the wind

this is how it began
when the grave would not rest
and peace was from us rent
to worms the world now rolls
rather than to the east

THE PRODIGIOUS FALL

at the moment
when I had begun
to forget myself
there together
in the crowd
the windows broke inwards
and the icy bows of evening
stretched across
our humored propensities
the personage of creatures
beaconed
at the shattered
glass panes

we all knew what would come next
and there it was,
the avalanche of dread
knowing what it is that they are
whom we must face this night
so our fear ran
with footsteps running
rushing... pounding...
for our very lives
in desperate abandon
lunging for escape
as though treachery
clung to our feet
and the way out
seemed further
with every step
already victims
fell at our heals
the evening cheer forgotten

this is our heart ache
falling upon the exits

at the doors
the street swung into view
the avenues
were a shadowed blur
laced in mist
and electric fear

I thought to look and so I did
back and over my shoulder
if a torrent could
be a thing to see
that is what I saw
in all its rush and collapse
a crashing deluge
pressing on our backs

they are frozen waters
beneath breaking ice
their teeth are arrows
their tungs are rusted knives

I thought to look and so I did
back and over my shoulder
frightening was her venom
a sour and sore mania
in this way the night upon us closed

FRAY OF ENTANGLEMENT

our hopes burn slow
as a campfire in the rain
and the wet and green logs
that resist the flames desire
to converge on their carbon rooms
the elemental organics
whose potential goads
press the wooden vats
and squeeze out the oils
and so it is that we our selves are beset
in a world that has run
head long into discord

for the night in its calm
magnetic balm
whose language
is its own distinction
is to us a certain ambassador
swaddling our concerns
in the buoyant flame of confidence
though the dark wall around us
will not by it self restrain
the harrow struggle
and the fray of entanglement
what persons will we be found to be
unfolds from our purposes
and what words we gather
to us our selves

for the vandals who crow
and gape at our living passage
are but fretful catacombs
whose morose electronics

smoke from the sullen ground
setting ablaze our strained foundations
of wood, hay and stubble
and so as what first was a smolder
under the causation of our undoing
grew to an underground burning
pulling apart our storehouse
with oxygen fueling the fire

I thought as many
that the government would avail
be it the W.H.O. or C.D.C. or our military
it seemed beyond belief
that anarchy could have so effortlessly
rushed into fill the void
the vacuum left
by our inability to respond

as such, the wood of our civilization
was not green

but easily
I think too easily
succumb the fire
our hopes
none the less
are not so loosely
dispatched

THE LONG END OF SUMMER

when all at once
and without our attention
civilization was tossed
shoveled into the fire
for what wide and unfolding furrow
should beneath us appear
as some inescapable and turning wheel
handing the world as it were
on a silver platter to the jackals
blood smeared faces of this
our waxing indian-summer
our endless hot, dour nights
whose lightening rod and prideful flight
has roused in us a mountain of dread
as though our harvest moon
were cast down into the sea
the tide there-in could all but boil
the waves eclipse the northern star

I turn my face to the sound of your voice
which breaks in me as the dawn
you have again proven
with your undying devotion to preservation
that we will not die today

for the enormous grim and gray cataract
whose whirl and winded torrent
will no doubt seem
a wide and covering cap stone
entombing any and all good we thought possible
but it was your call
that with hard steel hammers
we should fall with

the same grim weight
and break as we can
on the vast stone face
for such a covering
should entomb the dead and not the living
this was the assemblage and abstraction
which in time would again warm our blood
and dispel the icy bows back
to their billowing deep
the dead again rest
in their graves binding keep

for this alien august comet
which burst as a shimmering madness
above the still and serene mountains
and wove with its tail
a strange and unearthly terror
has with the great force of its venom
met not the vacancy of our defeat
but the anvil of our faith
and the grit of our community

in like manner I look again into the mirror
and purpose not the man I have been
our who, some might suppose,
I was born to be
but what person I need to be
against the dogs of blight
I choose to start again

HOT AUGUST NIGHTS

such as the point between us
bewildered turmoil to eclipse
the world that once was
threw our finger tips slip
and to us left one divided depose
with antagonism crouching at the door
our long hot summer flashes

the sun now burning our broken streets
the asphalt tar runs like a creek
so to this, the hold of our keep
can not defend
against what must rend
our heart like heat waves distorting
we have become undone
waiting to be reclaimed
recounting stories of a mender
who we is of the image of
here we set on the mantle of our hearts
your picture not to be forgotten

it lacerates at first dark
the incidental accolade
of our human alliances
must now endure
the press and fire
the lament and clamor
what has fallen to us as a hammer
treating metal as though it were clay

and so this our aggregate sum
our credible purpose that can only
stay the noise of chaos

by means maintained in the heart
and held in the mind
if it were faith by any other reason
it is our means of understanding
and how we relate to this cankered world

for certain sums shall but bear
the meta-distinctions
divers motion govern

and creatures slanderous black sentence to arrest

so we took the sick thing that it was
down to the river at sunset
and put down its trespass
into the world of the living

so shall by wasted means
the enemy seek us
those soundless stolen consorts
their steads do ravenous
under fatal canopy

before them is only a driving rain that takes away
awash in pernicious and pressing peril
while we lay still and endure the passing

and now what are we then determined to do

FOREST OF TORSOS

limbs attached to human stands
and forests of bodies
that fill the earth as woods that roll
out and down to the water edge

the soft machine that can not be explained
by tracing it through to its smallest parts
its great and costly fortune
springs forth with a word
its classical origin
is downwards causation
with delivery boys peddling fast
hard on the descent

the earth lay in the billowing sky
rolling over in a dream
she dreamt of men
and of eyes of perpetual winter

under the street lights
that no longer
hold back the dark
shadows unpackage
their grave new world
and the swollen thought
that strikes with infection
at identities inner door
presses without restraint
straight way to the heart
undoing what might have been

this damage has architecture
a buttress of the swarming

all those growing smokes
unfurling at our boarders
following determinations natural mechanism
breaking as waves against what is

the enormous order whose height
is tall as all the skies combined
will not endure for long this faction

if all the enmity in all the world
were brought to bare at once
its culmination could only be
a crackling furnace of disunion
drinking damage
lopping of its own feet
and at last falling
to the earth
that lay
in the billowing sky
rolling over in a dream
she dreamt of men
and of eyes of perpetual winter

AWAKE

an unfolding furrow
seemingly as wide as the earth
unfolding beneath our feet
was at first just the noise of events
but later swinging wide and far
made its sweeping undoing
to our neck of the woods
and there was no going back
to the lives we once were so invested in
the future, to which we had cast our hopes
has now become a dream
and the spreading damage
an awakening

to a new vision of what life will be
and what is possible for us
that walking death, if nothing else
are as crows that have come home to roost
and to assert their dominance
under whose anvil we have succumb
with the violence of extinction
under their talons
like a billowing breeze of damage
unending
pressing against
our closed doors

a cave with no bottom
whose darkness had escaped its mouth
and spilled out
over the wide open plain of the earth
our only respite
is our human capacity

to abstract for ourselves
the promise that the terror
of this wide and present moment
will not own who we are still becoming
in this way we put down
the infected barking from our ears
and erase from our eyes
what is the almost certain
dispatching of our hopes

though at the gates the shadows lengthen
and the cover of day light
slips from the sky
what sort of light
will keep us
is what still remains

the seeming absolute
of our grid now clipped
out global data net, cold and silent
and the collar of our coats
can not rise up high enough
against the evening air
what sort of light
will keep us
becomes the unpacking
of what we will hold to be
and by what hold
our keep will not be undone
when the grave of those hobbling swarms
press at our very door
their eyes locked in one circular thought
which drives the engine of their limbs
and renders them a force
of singular motion

carrying the worms of the earth
under their tung
cold as snakes
are these
rambling villages
who own no northern star
no judgment
no discretion

this their thoughtless option
as if nature were an evil lord
whose roots had reached up and tapped
the seat of existence
with one axiomatic rule
the in-escapable arrest of a law at work
commanding their feet in a path
that is a wondering
burning fire
that is never quenched
always wrecking
against the rocks
spraying acrid foam
into the air

we first knew they breached the yard
not from the sound of them but of the smell
one almost could cast a match
into their creeping vapor
and expect it to rush back to its source
in a jumping ball of fire

this, their smell, spiked our fear
not in mortal panic
but in certain fright
bright and clear and awake

DISCORD AS A FIGURE

on the 5th month, on the 5th day of the month
the afternoon light was waning
the sun above was looking
for a set of hills to slip beyond
discord it self was waiting
waiting for the shadows to lengthen
the world again to lay laden
in the evenings couched watches
the cooling air seemed to wail
those gravid figures seemed to shimmer
those animate tombs would here wonder
following the topography as it emerges
the incendiary amble of the dead
firing off volition as a arching circuit
beneath a crown of decay

I realize as we sat and watched the sun pass again
that we were watching the world die
the verdure of our kingdom
leaning into the flames
the marrow of our dominion pining
just as who can hold back the water
when once it spills forth ?
so it seems our end
flows forth before us
I expect a night to come
when it shall find the last of us
one of these nights
the shadows will lengthen
and will not end

I realize as we sat and watched the sun pass again
that we were watching the world die

it is not oblivion to which we fall
rather under weight we are pressed
a great and mounting weight
that we can no longer undo
against this knowing
we are out numbered
it flows forth
no one holds it back
is this to be our sorrow ?
or is this to be our courage ?
when the waves converge
into one discord of figure
is there a position left to us
in which we do not succumb ?
a world left to us
that is not lost ?

the crack of gunfire
has inaugurated this night again
and with it the cold and crisp air
with its visions of amorphous gray
steeps the whole of our perception
in the distinct and its host of particulars
here in the dark our sight might discriminate
and divide in certain selective
the figure of what is good
and the shelter of accuracy
to preserve the hold of the living
for the great and vast tent
turns not on the terror of emptiness
but upon the hinge pins of the crafted
and the values of the laudable
these have become our binding chords
the garment of our endurance
and the application of our violence
in a world thrown to the wolves

THE NONE EXISTENT

from within the woods and under the sea
the arms of the kraken have put forth
its blighting hands
an alien antagonism as from the deep
as though that abysmal place
where light never presses against
its cold stone ceiling
has by means unknown
loosened it self from the governing chains
and crawled from the darkness
lawless as the wilderness
its eyes lick the air
and see our bodies heat

what it saw was it self in all things
and so all things it sought to reduce
to pull back beneath the waves
back to the crushing black
to dissolve the world in its abrogation

it is an entanglement of discord
which has found passage into this world
has discovered marrow bones to walk on
the empty vessels of the dead
has become its new abandon
a thief in the haunted hills
walking amongst the trees
standing tall in its unknowing night
it is the smoke of fire
where there is yet no fire
a billowing blight ashing on the driving wind
this the none existent
to inhabit the existent

squatting under deaths dissolution
under its decomposing canopy
to move amongst the living
in unsympathetic action

its malcontent we thought was cruelty
but in time we had come to recognize
it was is truth
an envious worm
its poison pursuant to impale
the world of breath and life

for the darkness from which it had sprung
was also its inexplicable sorrow
this its weeping, this its screaming
with which there is no logic, no article or rule
no alien tung with which to curse
or pine against us
eyes only on this our gates
smoking against our very being
there is no plan on how to quench our hope
it only knows that this is what it will
as a deluge that overflows
a tsunami that breaches the wall

ambassadors it has sent
upon them is born the billowing
the wailing and wide breach
staring from the fathoms
within them is wrought the squall
the blast and bluster
in all the bite and pierce of ice and spray
awash in our atrophied and halted city streets
wondering our complexes
our dashed urban core

our leaning megalith
is now a great shadow
a wide and yawning eclipse
from which we must emerge

the world looked to me as something
wholly other than what I had known
for a time uncertainty mocked
crawled beneath my bed
moaned from my closet
my windows would only twist and distort
the world that had crashed before me
an unknowable night
held the indistinct, the irregular
the ambiguous dismay which left me languishing
grasping for what remains
of the real if real were still a thing
had the stars fallen from their height
bringing their weight to bare against the sky
squeezing the earth in the unbearable
there is no relief, no escape
the realization that in the end
we are intolerably outnumbered
pulses before my eyes
then drops from my sight
leaving me shell shock
in the unbelief of the moment
a moment that I can not shake
in questions of which I know
none of the answers
against the glistening
and terrible press
of this
the magnetic monster
casting its great

and dazzling shadow
a wide and yawning eclipse
from which
I must emerge

THE NEW SALT TRADERS

the hopes of our present circumstance
remain pressed down
held to the ground
under the weight and ravager
as though the torrent of storm bared down
straight way to our last resort

the unprecedented unraveling
of our modern fortunes
the unrealized promise
of a future which we thought boundless
was for many an impossible medicine to swallow

when the lights went out
one had the sense
that we had turned a corner
disease and misfortune
have always scratched at humanity
have always held some ground
like dogs at the tree line
but now they have gained the upper hand
whose revenge has been long brewing
drawing against us
a cataclysm for which
we had no context

so as it has turned, that is,
this days grievous sentiments
harsh and mean and uncaring
seems without purpose or reason
by what fault has this ruin been deserved
by what indifference did we stumble forward
into this dire furnace

this den of lions
with eyes on our marrow

what are we to do with this
how are we to respond in the face of such riot
unbeknownst to us, entropy had grown teeth
the teeth of a bear and the jaw of an anvil
against such things is our vexation
our lives adrift with no certain shore

what values can be attached
to the issue of living
when living seems reduced to base survival
how to live is yet applicable, ever arresting
the problem of being will yet discover
where my loyalties lie

it is a circle within a circle
an axis on which turning owes its motion
unpacking the issues involved
this, our new and modern salt trade
our stronghold amidst the rocks
seasoning the force of, for us, what remains
our eloquences that originates
with each beat of the heart
struggling not to dwell in desperation

and so our cubic rooms have emerged
from the salvage
those parts of our environment
of which we still might yield control
our curtains hang out in the bluster
whipped in the gusts that seam to be unending
the constant blowing that has camped
with us for days now

rendering our fires a rising whirl of tails
trailing in the blowing evening

what forces are left to us
amongst these our scavenged forms
unfold a new type of city in layers
shadows bend in and out of light
and conformed to photon verdure
fanning in the dark
where we move in between the tight channels
and rifts in the cliff face

the plague was depicted
with worms worn within
the commonness of the condition
spread like flies
walking on cold marrow bones
across the slow infected night
imploding motion uncovered
this new villain bore its own mass terror
debouched human is its weapon
attend to what ills ravage worn on the sleeve

these morose lions have brought
a cold and driving rain
against our once verdant hillside
saturating the earth in a deluge that in time
could not be held back
and so they fell upon us
the earth overturned beneath us

THE COMMON MAN

the mediocrity of the common man
whose casual and desperate tension
that once held its own
against the usual despair
has now succumb to oppressors we knew not of
for the songs that had lulled
us in a venal parade
have turned silent
our medicines have run dry
our once well mannered control
is in the mad house

on this hysteria the sun will rise
loosed ossuaries mob upon us fold
the gate of our ragged strengths
swing the heart ache
as our defenses they ford
agents of the worm
are at the door
the pressure is our undoing
as the locks give way
and the set bolts shear
for when they breach our hold
we have prepared no way out

what epistemological savages are we
having rendered for our selves
no efficacious action
having discovered at the last
how vulnerable we truly are
as the world turns west to the fires
the factions on us implode
they need only to find us unguarded

our keep without defense
there to spike our wanton liver
with teeth as knives
and the jaws of a hammer

THE DIVISION

had this diminishment not fallen upon us
with the form destroying weight of the sea
had its crashing thrust
not pulled our limbs beneath the waves
the absoluteness of our loss
may have been less bitter
our undoing less desperate
our collapse might not have resembled as it did
a cornered animal with only its fangs and claws
to keep from this its doom
was there no paint with which we might
mask the cruelty of our corruption
no gold leaf to change the mediocrity
of our clay vessels
against the gloom of this our gathering night
whose sirens have sent envoys
crashing the heart of our private securities
thieves that have spotted our secret rooms
and drew plans against all our casual ease
as though nature her self
had envisioned our demise
had gathered against us her blockade
her rampart and grappling hooks
in all things she rendered us exposed
wounding our pining metropolis
spiking our sure footings
with amaroidal burning
our last defense was in the end
what had mattered most

    the notion of absolutes
    becomes concrete
    in the face of absolute loss

the weight of ruin gave certain focus
to what in life was worth living
what worth might regain us a confidence
that is not subject to the walls of necrosis
that now divide our mortal campaign
what distinctive aspect might bare up
under the crush of dissolvent wreck

some would wag their heads at the ruin
curse and lament they cry
for God has dealt us
death and damage
despair and flee
for life is terror
and life is disunion

some that are with me
we hold in hope
a certain volition
that havoc can not crumple
in its cool, unsympathetic hand
the property beneath our tung
as it is not an unmeaning vacancy
nor an inane trivium

the consequence of living
is closer now than ever
in this way the day has weight
the values that remain have become material
and the word 'important' has become real
like the warmth of sunlight
that pushes away the fog
of a cool smoking earth
this our substantial loss
has turned on the hinge pin of conflict

and become our imperative
this our earnest principle
has become our keep
against the shadowed collective
whose marrow can grow no more blood
as they circle the singularity of disease
the seat of being botched
in this their animated death

oblivions chief is a ragged host
wondering the meadows and woods

where there is no path

no bridge

no crossing

THE UNENDING CONFLICT

to the extent that the world could turn gray
it in fact did

while the length and breadth
of all its indigenous color
its particular inherent pallet
still held intact
yet all seemed couched
in granite ash, in stone slate,
a thin cinereal smoke
gripping all the edges
ladening all the basins
in ever distinct aspect
though rains could not actually
swamp all the earth
or swallow the world
even so some how the stone face of the sea
has made our rivers flow backwards
rolling inland in a doleful cinder deluge

sere shade has become the weight of the world
our great vaulted roofs collapsed
the beams that held our halls aloft is fallen
our colonnades vexed and halted
has this abasement rendered
the world indiscriminate
has existence become neutral and ineffectual
our global metropolis lay prostrate
disorganized and exhausted
with civilization left
scourged and shot to pieces
is there not yet purpose
to which we are still citizens

order to which we still belong
might it have been that absolutes
were not the finery of invention
that meaning and significance
were not the illusionary facade
of our fabricated language

the dawn seemed to lift the dismal blanket
and spike the sky in shafts of gold
the sooty slate lid of morning twilight
could not diminish the rift
of day breaking on the horizon
as a man rising to stand upright
so the face of some ancient gilded king
whose look sent lucent fire
down upon the earth
rendering the load of some great colossal weight
the basis for standards
to which all other distinctions
owe their particulars

these are our mornings
eclipsing the indiscriminate dark
turning the disordered night
into the lucid and the definitive
the express object
of the certain
and the particular

laden, as yet, in the ruin,
of this our immense collapse
worn as a garment
on the body of our world

an old, ragged shamble of us

whose moth eaten tares and scour
do not change the fact that with every day
the discriminative nature of living
is new as the day it was born

no fallen wall
which our hands had piled
is evidence to some
cosmic nihilism
some axiom of abandon
on which the world turns
that this apocalypse
should issue us license
to lapse to our most base self
under the auspice of survival
is not consonant with
the discriminative light of day
in which we move and see
on this awareness I am awake
and from this distinction
distinction becomes
what I can touch
and handle and process
against the ash and terror
of a world in havoc

THE VULTURE

if the sea could stretch
her weighted depths
across this haunted valley
I would there be banded
in her binding keep
kept secret from the clamoring limbs
which have swallowed this city
in certain sorrow
they are cowed sirens
who seek only to swallow whole as hell
all my ardent provisions

are they not envious worms
who would wait no more
for caskets to succumb to earth and rain
and so their identity now animate
in the sorrows of men
seeking as wolves
with eyes on
our very marrow

I can not, will not fall
beneath their talons
those magogs
those pounding crypts

I can not, will not fall
and they will not own
what I will defend
though this night will rend
our hearts as breathing flames
this night with its wind and rain
and sparks that climb on channeled drafts

the flames will inhale the air

I can not, will not fall
so I must cast down their ruin
those infected locusts
and brood of madnesses
to them reason is a stranger
so they lodge but a breath
from certain tombs
an accord of collapse
with no northern star
or realities mirror
so vultures watch and gather
where their bodies lay

THE HEART

on mantles born beneath the ribs
and below the shoulders
the essential dispositions
couched in rhythmic procession

twisted and spooked
like the earliest part of morning
when it is not day nor is it night
ideas throw roots within
the object of their information
moves as the assertion of forces
reaching for the mind with wires
pounding on the hearts private room

so the thought will emanate
growing cortextual buttresses
all those acquired constitutions

this 'the machine' it bleeds

the machine it breathes
sending forth its soft, pliable wires
palpable as the earth it self
modifiable as clay

the air has texture
like granule smoke
their arms reach in
riding the thoughts of decay
which grow inside
the force of motion
with hands
that look

for my throat
lodging inside
volitions
secret
retreat

they are horses racing down
eating the earth like determined men
limping in ruts of their own damage
their feet held to the fire

the hammering process goes on
finding reason in every circle
and in every subsurface
those thoughts which informed
the place which the earth abides

RISE

what balm or aid might turn back
might quell the ill volumes
awash at all our stirring gates
had the rumors not spoke of fallen capitals
our primary metropolises bending into the flames
we would have suspected the worse none the less
for the breach of all our gilded trust
was with certain venom
as an arrow to the liver
our hours now numbered

have we not yet succumb to the ravages
this pining undoing
of all our organized invention
our stakes now puled
from the ground
of this our bleeding earth

I would close my eyes to the press
still the glare of the furnace was blazed
upon the inner nerves of my sight
reaching in with twisting limbs
to press against the keep of my thoughts
so my eyes I squeezed shut
closed against the blast and wail
so I would erase from my vision
the complaint and doleful cry
away from the governing hold
from the beating heart
and the emotional sum

to breath and collect and gather again
the notion that my hopes are not yet lost

that I have not yet
fallen off the face of the world
the leviathan stayed
the barking dogs of blight
have retired for the hour
back into
the gravitoid of sorrows
a world blinded
in the narrows

feeling for the wall
as the blind listening
for clues to what is
holding my self
up against
the corner stone
the principle corner
has become my resort
with curtains closed
I imagine
there is
no more
ruin

A NATURAL RULE

the air was still
steeped in walnut and water
the wheat and the fodder
and what seemed to be
fires beyond the hills
turn to dusk and the setting sun
folding as a nebula
beneath the magnetized mantel

the wound is our pining city
our dissolution beneath the vast realm
which fans out in great arching spans
turning north
rooted in axis
as some colossal king
irreducible
incorruptible axiom
foundational without release
there is therefore
no ambiguity
no nihilism
no meaninglessness

forced and unnatural mentality
is want of value
and the form of mien invention
twisted and wrestling
biting at the earth
seeking what new drug
can ware again the mask
and the desperate bid to exist

THE ZOMBIES

some how morose larva made their home
in the words with which we built our lives
the leaning structure
which succumb in slow defeat
to the elemental absolution
of what turns out to be
most essential after all

BESIEGED

days, months into this grim global stone age
it became clear, ever so clear
if ever there was a thing
that was plane to see
it was the simple fact
that there would be no recovery
and from this we would not restore

it is our great misfortune
that such events could so undo
could so pin us to the ground
we would be down for the count
except there is no count
and there is no referee
and there are no rules

close your eyes but nothing changes
you will watch the world die
you will watch this strange new day
eclipse what was with an unending eclipse
what is this frightful dawn
that threatens us with extinction
that rolls upon us
as a dividing faction
cutting in pieces
our hold on life

our heart has
all at once stopped
is there a shelter
is there a passage back
to what we once knew

if we close our doors
against the division
and in our thoughts imagine
that the end is not an object
baring down on our camp
and the rain again is dreamy
and life again is new

THE ADVOCATE

fear as fear it self
has extended to us
the object of discord
the commerce of bane havoc
has bathed our course

thus this certain nemesis has rewarded us
emptiness for our uselessness
hopelessness for our dissolution
as it has turned to be
our capacity to solve
has proved a miserable comfort

fear as fear itself
has forced us down
put us in the ground
has extended to us
the arms of the grave

is the cosmos so indifferent
that our world should turn to blight
has not the anthropic sky
afforded some remaining provision
some last path of resort
a way out
of these
bleached badlands

was there not once
in bands of betrothal
in chords of our youth
against the wide gate of possibility
an advocate to which death would flee

THE METROPOLIS UNDONE PART 1

shafts of sunlight cut
through the skeletal high rises
rendering the clefted avenue
in braced brightness
shadows pushed to the edges
in ebonized eclipse
charging the rubble ablaze
in burnished, arid, volume
holding the remorse
of this wreckage at bay
that for the passing hour
the stark garden of debris might stand
in its own sharp beauty
the weight of its broken concrete
its smoke stained steal limbs
its shattered pristine pile
warming in the morning sun

at the foot of these weather carved towers
the remaining hulk of automation growing
the new vegetation of rust and ginger blight
deterioration is the new eco system
hydrocarbon; yellows and greens
pool under the cool awnings
of folded blocks
dusted in cement lime

mainly it was the gutting rampage of fire
that first exposed
these megaliths to the ravages
gas explosions cracked their skin
and opened their inner systems
to the task master of water and weather

the freezing of endless winters
railed at their milk fed bones
and found the porous surrender of atrophy
undermining the trusted columns

these are our vapid fields
the great vacancy
of these hollowed blocks
has become metaphoric of our own undoing

unfolding before us
as a megalithic jungle
of ambling and treacherous courses
which meander indiscriminately
through the rubble

the late afternoons bring winds
that swell in the avenues
and whistle in the open
face of the leaning towers

evening crawls across the monstrous walls
at times the presence of night
amongst the stone columns
was steeped in an obsidianic weight
palpable and present

at others the black face of the structures
seemed but holes in reality
angular juts of negative space
standing high into the evening air
one might pass into these holes
and not come back
have we spent too many years in this place?
I have begun to wounder

how much of my self
has been lost to the holes

what dwelling might remain
was in growing conflict
with the hazard of such a place
great shards of glass regularly fell
as the sheer of the super structures waned
foot paths amongst the heap
were never sure

under the press of time and weight
the mass was ever falling
congealing into a gathering ruin
so the nests of our community
that remain are spars
like outcroppings of verdant life
in a wide open dessert
existence here is forged
in the crevices and crags
a loosely bound crew of scavengers
we are survivors
we hold what ground we can
dug in to what amounts to
strongholds amongst the heap
places of vantage
up in the network and lattice
of super structure above the streets
where at best one might know
what unexpected threats
might have wondered
into the rampart of avenues below
be it the living or the dead

A METROPOLIS UNDONE PART 2: HOW WE CLIMB DOWN

what else could we have done
as though the suns radiation did strike us
and pull us apart at the seams
spiking our blood in discord
disease has become the face
of this our ruptured vessels
breaking on the rocks
crashing in the spray

the grief of what had gone down
the plagues, the rotting money, the wars
the ultimate inability to respond
to any of it in any meaningful manner
has become our hammering process
has left in its wake
a people ghosted, shell shocked and shattered
somber as orchards which no one attends
the cultivation that returns to the disorder
of natures first order
while alas we try to put back together
or discover what chaos now means
how to live with what now is

some people I see from time to time
it seems to be that this for them
can only culminate in their own withdraw
for over this cliff they fall
to flee from the cruel rabble
in utter retreat from what
the world has become

silence is this their pale gloom
white washed and worn on the sleeve
for what has befallen is the impossible
to the unimaginable there is no answer
for in this the good
the bad
the rich
the poor
all have been caught together
in this net of liquidation

indiscriminate
unsympathetic
without distinction
the whole sale misfortune
of so many
caught in the headlights
blinded by its rush and roar

the day, though young, was flaming
and the winds were not waiting
for the grittier part of afternoon
in order to dissolve the rubble born dust
into a whirling dirty fog
I wanted to get on with my business
before the air became too unbreathable
and my cough would start spiking
the bottom of my throat again
so I gather my day pack and goggles
and the rags I use to tie to my face
to hold back the air born cloud
of particles and fibers
from pressing into
what is left of my lungs

and make a way down
from the hoveled residence
a nest of yellow chemlight glow
a home in the dank an dim
descending what remains
which wound down
in an eight landing spiral
that was mainly bathed in darkness
except for the faint glow that fell in rays
which beamed down from damage above

knowing each step as though acquainted
to climb them in absolute blackness
requires becoming tacitly accustomed
to its individual parts
its particular damage
its loose ruble on the steps
its bent and broken handrail
which juts out, impeding the passage
with now almost little hesitation
bounding to the bottom
the lowest most exit is flooded
only on rare occasion
do I bother wading though its muck
preferring the ruin of the lobby
now the grand, structural glass shattered
its metal frame buckled
its ceiling facade collapsed
its floor cluttered in the bulk of all
that had made its way
down to its ground zero
now weeds and blight
clung to its open wounds
filling in where
roots could take

a foot hold
it was by way
of the rambled strewn lobby
that I make my passage
through to the streets

A METROPOLIS UNDONE PART 3: WHAT THE DEAD CAN NOT FORD

In the open the jungle of the overturned
the undone, the displacement of all
that was man made
lay in blended rupture
spilled out and recumbent

to walk amongst it was to ever turn and twist
to step over, to avoid
the straight and direct were gone
the level and the ample gate of walk ways
now smashed into discord
the scale of such upheaval
its shadow and weight
was breathtaking

to watch the light of day
fold and unfold across the mass
of this civic implosion
was an event in it self
the foreignness of its environment
seemed to belong to some were else
as though what was mile-high
had dislocated it self and swung
in the most irregular of downward motions
bringing with it some part of the roof of the sky
rendered the ground in the alien and unearthly

we walk as though
having passed this way
enough times to glean
its residual experience

as a mental imprint
thus crossing its irregularities
in the meditation of muscle memory
seeming to mount the clutter
with the least degree of attention
and the indifference of those who expects
to see nothing new
or as those who wouldn't
care if they did

the sun already has climbed up onto the rooftops
cutting down through the wedges in broad shafts
and bathing the wounded hull in burning day
the residence of the ruins
dwell in the most formidable structure
making a hold from what to us is left

the calling of the broken walls
was not for the sake of living in the past
nor merely to scavenge the refuse
rather it was the protection
which this shifting colossus afforded
protection not as much from the antagonism
of marauders or anarchist gangs
though holding the advantage
against such didn't hurt
it was the blockade which the rubble amounted to
that held in repose
the infected mobs of the dead
though their marrow be cool as the crypt
yet their limbs ever unresting
hover as a siege against the walls
of this great and pining edifice
it is the complexity
of negotiating

this insipid capital
of broken concrete
that renders its passage
a perplexity
the whole of it
a sort of mote of rabble
this has become
the keep of the living
a home in the castles
canopies above

WHAT IS LEFT TO US

bane forms in morose rags
that fill what once was the avenues
now more meadow than boulevard
on patches where tar asphalt
has not yet succumb
they gather and collect
by a process of gravitation

as the lengthening shadows of afternoon
they are as crowds that overflow the room
pressing on the walls
spilling out of the attic
were death a king
they have become deaths new dominion
wondering the streets
as a perpetual fog
rolling slowly on the wind
damage on the breeze
crows follow this new strange procession
scavenging what they will
the house on the hill is burnt to its posts
reduced to a pinnacle of ruin

so we avoid their dour and grim islands
their cloisters are meadows of thorns
we choose to stay clear
we walk at a distance
which renders us unknown
in the cloud of their unknowing

we have the guns
they have the numbers
has nature her self

sided with their clamor
in the mirror has she beheld
her grave determinism
her natural law
seems to have fallen
to their cruel lot
leaving us to wonder
what betrayal is this
has mother earth preferred
death over life
are these maggots
the apple now of her eye
eating up our fortunes
as locusts in the gain fields

with language we describe in terms
the notion with which we intend
to hold our course together
we choose not to fall
under this their extreme ravage

a regime of monsters
have found their way
to our store house and keep
the hills have forgotten us
the world has turned against us
as a fickle mistress
her heart to us no more aligned

with language we describe in terms
the notion with which we intend
to press into tomorrows
fortuitous and secret hold
we choose to gaze into the mirror
of our spotless and seraphic hope

and remember the world not as it is
but as it might yet be
not by the amorphous value
of our varied subjections
but by the certain abstract object
of that which is in an accord
and at this we are certain
that death shall have no dominion

THE SQUALIDS

the steep of night crept
undone, no sun
the streets in wind are swept
ill beginnings of what seemed our end
for the moment forgotten for enough away

opposite of noon
blustered and broomed
ground floor windows shattered
the dead in rags are tattered

curtains hung out snapping
crowing in laden air
at the corner past the walk
that wondered between the residence
was the popping of arcing wires
up in the busted street lamp
there on the corner
throwing sparks in the gusts
tailing in the wind

broken, wounded town
the sound of it all around
the bluster, the billow, the breath
ghosted paper mills tall like trees
seed the air with ink
steeped in the approaching rains

beside the great and solemn sheer
rising high beyond the clouds
beyond and upwards and boundless
the magnificence to which words owe their handle
consonant with this

evenings slow fanning notes
soaked, spoke to the august
and noble word
as silver cleaned in the fire
this ring of portent to ware
one wedded band fresh as air

long beside the tree line
the dark
the park
the exact act
of resting an ear
to the sound
of words
funded
by certain
underwriters
a coarse of witness
whose line has gone out
in every
and all four corners
in the shadows
and in the light
cool as calm
cold camouflage

beyond the sentiment is steeping
the garment breathing
gathered about as solaces eminent hold
a world now dosed in feeling
the feeling was separating
fanning original
dark on the vista

PERSPECTIVES

Perspectives are kept in bottles
ageing, metamorphicly emerging
with an oath to origins

seeing the world
having a basis
in what is known to be
by perspective

pining at the emotional sum
of what lay secret
steeping within

so children are debtors
they owe them selves
to what we've shown them

it becomes with age an image held close
the pulse and rhythm....
of, for them, what is

always seeing what they seek to see
or until by at what time or place
it should be by some means become clear
that there are choices
and that our primal oaths
are not absolutes

what is far is also near
the emotional sum of reason

THE PICTURE

whom I look to know
in this way look up to see
to crown the image and tie the chord
which I hold to be
and so hold
close to the heart

a picture to slowly erase the scars

THE NARROWS

from the narrows
the sound that I heard
de-constructed in the hearing

in passing by the stairs that wound down
that turned away from seeing
one had the sense of damage
spreading as smoke
descending as ropes from our eyes

asps could dwell in what might tell
the talk that carelessly speaks
de-constructing in the hearing

as I passed, the structure lay in ruin
turning in the leaning noon
what portent will stir
the subtext of our devices
that spell the order of our disposition

and the breeze would blow billows in the night
breathing on our uncertain windows
mobs of horses running in ranks
if you strike them they are not wounded
they over turn the earth
in limbs chaotic
reaching for the foundation

my eyes can loose their color
robbed of their provision
the gifted room onces had
bleeds out in the debt
as I remembered it

the grasses leaned into the heat
our meadow of consequence burning
undone and drawing off the bowls
in a room dominated by disease
the dead have legs to carry them
they break from the long night air
as cold as the earth
wondering the city parks at dawn
those haunted headless hallows

to ascend this ravine
our family bonds must
belong to the narrows

B MOVIE MONSTERS

these are no B movie monsters
these are no innocuous macabre
their grim alarm is here
they are at the doors
pressing at our gates
grinding at our heals

a den of asps coiled in the eyes
one part has arrested the whole
has invaded the sum of mind and sight
has eaten the human good
in a dragging limp

a lurid identity has grown
with spanning vines
which spread in ghastly function
tapping at essential nerves
lodging in secret rooms
of personal vestige
smothering the better angles
of our nature

these are no B movie monsters
these are no harmless creeps
no toothless dogs
these morose companies
these botched silhouettes
their mouths are as abandon
voicing maggots and worms

a den of creeps
whose strength is their numbers

THE CITY WITHOUT LIGHT

I see only electric light
the city arching through my eyes
the avenues can lead to nothing certain
the streets commerce all but ruin
those ordered lots
and store front blocks
have pined in shattered disunion

those hopes could not hold
this world in stable provision
could not bind our prodigious securities
in sustaining progress

so all our silver were but plated clay
shattering under the shear
force of misfortune
how thin the vainer of corporal benefits
and so the rolling hills
have turned upon us

so the prodigious economy is broken
and the march of ditches swells
growing with the tide
dragging us through

when I saw the procession
I realized what I was seeing
those body parts on parade
wrapped in black plastic
after the car wreck

and the haunted interstate
merges with the darknesses

that follows the setting sun
death will have no dominion
so such is our desire to prevail
running on exists
in certain volition

THE PARK

to the park after dark
the wheels of evening turn
above the atmosphere holds us
below the grass
flush with dew
breathes fog at our ankles
and makes the darkness seem charged

on the swing set the stars are closer
the haunted streets seem further
the wind is waiting with us
until the hour does pass

was it the ground that broke ?
like a spider nest
spilling its innards
hatching its organism
out onto the verdant earth

is this natural when
corruption is what spills out ?
can the earth bare up a monster ?
hands that climb up from the ground
out into the verdant night

the twisted men with wounds on the sleeve
and the eyes of trees that are dry
whose leaves do not return
after the colder seasons

was it from the smoking ground
in the park when the sun was not
that figures loomed

like some gaping cave
it is not enough to loath those ruins
we must belong to something more

THE DOOR

To the court, the old men resort
as they cross the street
when the sun is at its apex
above the great blue chamber
the alley was full of strangers
who bare shadows in their palms
holding the roots that already break the surface
and send their primary stocks

and at the court the door was locked
against the press
and stress of what will come
unfolding even as our fingers slip
the grip we thought was firm as nails
pulled from our fastened set
our curtains rent
under the blue chamber
whose ambassadors spell torrents
in the downpour that would follow

all those hollow passengers
have gathered at the edge of town
their shadows invert
casting long columns into themselves
fracturing on each step
the hold of thought
which spills as the object
of their invention
unstable and substantial
their doors are locked against the press
and the stress of what will come

the old men that have crossed

knew the locks where set
so carried they beneath their vests
in inner pockets hold
lock picks in order to spin the tumblers chamber

so to those who thought their hold would stay
by a dead bolts fastening firm as nails
gasped when the doors blew open
in all the light and the rain and hail

THE MOON

the moon is watching
our world turning
our broken glade of earth
leaning into the fire

i wish you did not see us this way
the sight of this our fright
grief has unpackaged
what we are made of
has discovered the naked form
has chased us down
to our forlorn and halted ends

do you not see how our heart is torn
bending under the weight
under the fading light
folding in on us this fading golden sky
as the sun sinks we see you rise

standing up on the edge of the earth
you are white as snow
we are white as ash
you have discovered us here again
i wish you didn't have to see
our eclipse into the night

the hours that follow
bring strange lament
the dead no longer at rest
in their earth bound shroud
they have become standing shadows
that move into the dark fog of evening
owls have noticed them

emerging from hollows
like messengers from the mire
trafficking their grim complaint
that their grave rest is gone
their crypt overturned
spilling them out
to seek revenge
on the world of the living
to stagger across the earth
in the glowing moon light
the night sky is turning
leaning into the fire
fanning the passing of fortune
as you look on

THE ROAD

the road was lined with trees
which held for us only the perception
of what was most immediate
and not what lay beyond
for the night was thick as ink
and only what lay above
informed our indigenous alcove
the forever intruding sky
and the star light on its descending columns
dropping into my sight
clefting the vertical edifice of space
and time which seemed its prisoner
and the bleak abandon of my nocturnal earth
was a stranger to its larger environment
for all the isolation of our grim disaster
held us blinded as a dear in the head lights
while the noise of our dismemberment
seemed to us the only axis
by which to describe what is
for power it would seem
belongs to the oppressor
and terror it would seem
has made its dwelling
in the mouths of the dead
rolling forth as some form destroying deluge
piling as it were
as the walls of the deep
looming just beyond the trees
that lined our rural road through the night

so we walked in silence
almost with eyes closed
as to hear what sound might tell

of what aliens of life
might lumber beyond
in the gross and amorphous dark
should the company of stars we hope
watch over this treacherous night
might know for us some safe and secret passage
by which we might escape again
the antagonists who traffic
the grave as an open highway
a wide and open course whose exposure
from which we must remain withdrawn
whose implosion we must defect
and remove our selves from their devices
for at their table is damage
dining as ravenous dogs

for them there is no northern star
no passage to the day beyond
for when the sun climbs
and fills the atmospheric height
the dark stays with them
as worms stay in the ground
as death and life are not equal
so with prejudice we gladdy
return them to their rest
that the stars may again
watch over where they have fallen
and north again be north

WHAT LIGHT LOOKS LIKE

for the bright and emotional sum of light
spiking our sight in electric focus
sharp and distinct
like the anvil of our eyes
was folded into absolute clarity

though dark as dark it self
had at one time seemed to touch the sky
and infuse nature
with its fossilized primordial ink
its coal covering can not remain
for light is its undoing

with seeing we have seen
the voltage and the sparks
sourcing our emotions
weighting the hold of feelings
and the discriminative quality
of this our divisible apprehension

this has become our desire to preserve
and for the cause for which
reason has embellished

for in the farthest north
above the ice and sea
explosions resound in the silent vastness
as though the crafting hand
would fold the suns into a periodic table
and squeeze water from the crucible
for absolutes one might conclude
have been attended to
the particular and the unique

owe their assignment to the discriminative
and the discerning hand of composition

so it seems such a constructor
of things seeming unbearable
as though the spilling out of the seas
so also the simple and the serene
is seeded in sentiment
sending roots into our lives
in the same way our mathematics
is consonant with what we see to be

A STREET AT NIGHT

could I not pass
through your narrow corridor
your haunted evening streets
whose distant light disrupts my red eyes

shafting the night air in white, silent shards
splintering through my swollen eyes
bleeding at my halted doors
tapping at what is possible

portent and value
from which there was no escape
cracks the wood and sends sparks
up into the cool, humid night
I close my eyes to see the orange coals
still rise in my sight
I see their embers dissipate
in the swaths of shadowed scapes

the evening smoke swings
across the edges of what is knowable
what particulars lend their roomers
the ideals softly spoken

of directions which are narrow
pressed, as some moral weight
have I lived in caves all my life
to only now see the expanse
the realism and her rose goads
a winded dominion fanning the fires

to this end I am given time to unfold
to unpackage who i'll choose to be

the volume of your keep fills all the ends
like water that fills all the world
with its swaddled table and finest china

CAUTERIZE

I could only look and see
the aghast macabre
as water that pours out
can not be born back

through a blustered field
clothed in summer azure sun
I am calm but I am afraid
the pressure of chaos
seems not far
their fires already jumping
through the winded grass
all marked in the sight of
spooked mortal panic

I could only look and see
through the trees
the stand of thicker shadows
that seem to flow down in waves

my keep is not my own
and I am not alone
against those vultures
who prowl like dogs
at my very boarders
reason is a defense
in the sunlight of my volition

I could only look and see
the spray and foam of crashing bonds
what have held them in locked signature
a mind captured in the swarm

so their handle
their construct
will burn
in all our corners
in every home
with families and friends
bereft of sight
fanning the fires
of this their aberration

drained from the heart
is the capacity
to discern
to divide
the pieces of the form
and so these evening ills
haunted and limping
disease as fabrication
supposing the worst in men
this school of the inane
we must be the death of the party
we must cauterize and put it down

the decay was in the heart
the disease was in the mind
riding on infected thoughts
born of forces which excrete pressure
pushing in on the hold within
infected thoughts, infected eyes

'greetings' I say from the gallows
how is it that this table
has torn my world apart
these neurological spikes
limping forwards to what end?

THE DEATH OF A MONSTER

our shattered hopes and broken dreams
can not long occupy our ardent love
for with blood and horror
the forces that undo
have set the sight of their arrows
on our very fortunes
they would as wolves
divest our very being
for the great length of our volume
must be a fire within
for our very lives
we will over come
though the walls of the sea
should stand against us
and inundate all our provision
with wires and venom
electrolyzing with panic
taring at our bowls
feasting on our bones
for the mouth of their envy
seeks to consume unending

there was a time and there was a place
when I beheld the great step
which they took into my world
for when they took from my own
and when they devoured
as a monster of violence which can not me halted
I was for a time without answer
I could not respond to this their war
though the sea should scream against me
swallowing whole as hell
"you and all that is yours"

this she bellows
this she cries but I have had enough
of her hell at my heals
for the voice has a tung
and a tung can be cut out
and her tung will know its end
against such things I will consume
and I will destroy
though destruction role forth
as a covering and rolling storm
but to this I am what I believe
and against this ruin
I am no more subject

we are a communion
we share a common mother
purpose is at our table
shared and passed around
we are what we believe
for the sea is in volume crushing
we are yet a breach and breaking jetty
against our rocks she can only foam
she can only spray
for what great and gray creature
might with hight and power
be anything more than a moment in time
destroy with your calamity
destroy with your wave
your passage is a loaded siren
a screaming alarm
your pressure is a vast weight
in time we will out last
not on our own merit
for the ground of our stay
whose shadow is cast

over the whole length
of joy and calamity
of triumph and grief

though the alarm of the massacre
is born on arms which reach inwards
our windows broken
our homes sacked
and with blood and terror
and the fangs of a creature
that I might other wise fear
and a creature that I might other wise hate
though they scream at me
though they burn at my soul
at this I answer
with a bullet to the head
for the dead fall dead
and the grave says enough
and the morrows monster must cease
and with an answer to this terror
I must respond
for their siren is but flesh

WHEN HOPE SLIPS FROM OUR GRASP

when death no longer has a covering
life is no more what we thought to be
for the earth will grieve
the earth will grind
turning over under pale skies
beneath over turn their grave keep

it is an electric betrayal
when our dearest hopes
our certain claim on life
is halted in the innocuous
and stopped cold by the indiscriminate
and the burning blight of a grim mob
over turns all that we took for granite
throwing molotovs onto our wooden capital

how quickly memory lets go
of these our expectations
though our justification
once seemed without question
those assumptions now thwarted
and now too soon pine
into the folding day

the wind it howls
the wind it cries
the ghastly and disposed
on haunted limbs now walk the night
spreading as smoke to every corner
shadows have stepped into bodily form
how shall we give them no quarter

how shall we dispatch their worm filled flight
back to the hollows
back to where death does dream
O roll back their wave
to their proper keep beneath

THE HAMMER

her skull was a storm
when the dead wrapped in cellophane
pressed their matrix of grief
up through the cold earth, wet with night

the black cylinders
of gun powder fire tubes
whose crisp grit popped and jumped
under the snap of twigs and sticks
on the forest floor
the electric bonds
shot across the skin on the ground
with the spreading arms
of angular lightning
burning a path through the trees
and turning the heart of the forest
into black vinyl

we thought that only if
our words had wings
they might beat back
like bombarding hawks of prey
the spreading infested ink particulates
that now lodge under the ridge beam
of mens shoulders
and beneath the housing
of soft-wired-eyes

they could no longer make the sound of men
in the storm of this their swimming discord
swinging the heart ache
and her head was swimming
with the those color photos of adrenalin

pumping in vascular alarm

when the dead crawled from their tombs
like swimmers stepping up out
of the lake at night
their inked silhouette
were too restless
for the arms of their graves
when she looked and saw
she knew her heart was now a hammer
rushing gun metal through her members
sending time into its new slow motion passage
this, she would learn
as her means to an end

FABRIC

we run by numbers
across the uneven earth
the emotional force of our intention
breaking in pieces the demotion

they swallow whole as never full
chewing at our steps
we are not thwarted in their noise
this their dismembering clammier

we fall like hammers
on those diseases
in the course of time
this is our effect
taking back the earth in paths
that have been before
in ways to which we return
pushing forward a new order
shaping a buttresses and causeways
that turn upwards into
an ancient and wide avenue
pulling abstraction from the boundless resource
from one who fights with ardor

the sky is woven
a loom unfolding the macro-verse
with the weight of numbers
drawing particular attribute
across the face of the evident
a plumb line from of above
from which all abstractions
derive their use and meaning
the fabric of what is
the thread and hook
the binding chord
of a garment

JUST ANOTHER MORNING

the gravid collectives
that gather as some sort of grim weight
mull with the disunion
of ghastly alien structures
against them our calm is a weapon
our calculations divide what scourge might gape
to roll back the wake of this
those moorish ambling macabre
with no voice they do not speak
the sepulcher beneath
as dark as dark is bleak

we keep our nights not in the open
turning away from the exposer
and preferring rather the covering
of what shelter the rabble might afford
until the architecture of pining ruin
passes with the wind
by morning the bluff at the end of the street
has collected all manner
of refuse the blowing might carry
and the bodies of the deceased
who loiter as trash from the sea
driven into an alcove by the storm
they have no compass to recover their bearings
so as to find their way back to their graves
for their tombs have shut
their doors against them
while some strange electric maggot
lodges in the seat of their
once governing judgment
so they are adrift
hungry to avenge this their curse

their exile into a world
in which they no longer belong
so with the rising sun they become agitated
the dark no longer a buffer
against their unknowing
we dispatch them again to their crypt
forcing open the door that was shut against them
we then collect their remains
and loose them with fire
into the morning air

this is not our reclamation
this is not how we right the wrong
this is the business of clearing our area
and maintaining what is ours

THE CAMPFIRE

for solace was a sentiment
whose ring rang for hours
settling all the enigmatic sorrow
into kindling and fuel for the fire
as such we could spend the day
throwing heap to the pile
drawing off the refuge on grim baggage
the dry and the broken combustible floor
which lay strewn as a wooded ramble
at the forests feet

so when the day would fold
and relinquish its hold
on the great sky
the spark would smolder
the slight of breeze would gather
and stir the flames
into a growing force
hungry for air

and so the woods would bend
the tall hold of timber would stand
and enclose the silent speed of light
shafting the shadows in shards
breaking the night like glass
beckoning the throne of death
to come wondering through the trees
wondering as ghosts
who could not escape the dumb weight
of their dead bodies
and so the divide of life and death
is kept as a seat of misfortune
in the unnatural state of animation

as moths to the flame

so their mob would gather
and we would close their open tomb
with a single bullet to the head
and drop their blighting bag of tissue
into the consuming pier

this we would do to clear the surrounding land
to clear the earth of its grim complaint
and restore some measure of control
over our indigenous environment

THE GUN

should the portent
of ghastly antagonists despoil
should they fall upon us as a wave
they have now surrounded us in their steps
their chords encompass as the arms of a thicket
the darkness of waters and thick clouds
have gaped in a yawning collision

upon this great and black rift
we will not fall
though the earth scream
that this is our end

projectile case sacked in propellant
couched behind the cylinders ejection port
where the cartridge is loaded into the breech
fire powder held in packaged casements
serves the function
of imparting velocity to the projectile
our bullets cut the air with crisp whistles
exerting penetrating traumatic stresses
on the objects they hit
the energy is then dissipated in the wound track
by this means our will to preserve is exacting
casting ballistics as a wall against the torrent
by this we dislodge the force of terror
animate in the victims host bodies
those diseased crowns possessed in unrest

as though an ever dark and haunted forest
held in the cool of perpetual shadows
were to congeal and concentrate
and were to focus its disdain

with grief and sodden mire
and raise from its rotting bowls
a swarm of infestations
hacking the organisms core constructs
to give arms to abandon
to set loose its rogue agents
to wonder as a crowd of marauders
into the camp of the living

and so upon their dead chords
our cross hairs fix
we drop them until they are no more
breaking the spiritless cavity
of their black cataclysm
in a spatter on ink and flesh
ending their haunting
in finality by which we have found this
our strengthening rest

PART 2
THE DEFENDERS

THE DEFENDERS

we are restless while the monsters wait
through the trees we can hear the river
dropping through the land
the warm afternoon air holds the sound
as a child's sleep chiming

but when the evening comes crawling
the sound of water is a cataract in the black
for the antagonists are as wolves
who hunt in packs
and use the covering of dark
as a camouflage and trojan horse
pine caskets once held them
now the cool night projects them
into our restless holds

we use to sleep in abandon cars
until we realized the steamed windows
was a tell of our living breath
and the dead would gather
as vultures where the body lays

now in cars we take to the roads
and scavenge petrol as we roll
from one haunt to the next
in every quarter the windows are broken
and the perpetual every green of blight
has pressed its dominion deeper
into what once belonged to us

though the suburbs have fallen
to the ceaseless marauding meadows
the cars are ours

we take them where we will
we choose the ones we want
and draw from their utility
when the sound rolls along the road side
the world will know that we are not yet done

death has made chaos its trust
the faceless and aimless its home
we have made volition our handle
by which to distinguish our selves
from the overflowing riot
of dismembering decay

they pursue us in their wandering droves
a gang of pulsating masses
that cling as blight clings to ruin
as the moon clings to the night
before it passes back to the shadows
and the world a phantoms meadow

from them we once ran
now we live in avoidance
of their grim grinding gore
for our hold is acumen and reason
theirs is disunion
ours is concord and consonance
ours is agreement and chorus
for we have chosen the discriminative
and the eye of the explicit
for our faith is selective
and we punctuate what is

for the world we know is knowable
and terror we perceive is possible
so we select the particular

and arm our selves with rigor
for the world has seemed to us unfriendly
its cataclysm a trespass
to snuff out our happy life
and throw us down in disrepute
and make of us the ordinary
the insipid and innocuous
compost they would make of us
but we will have none of it

and so the river we can hear
the sound bubbles between the forest stands
and crashes in the open field
in the night it is an opiate
whose audio resonance
crosses over into my sight
and becomes a thing I can see
with the rest of what the dark can tell
and the soft sounds that form a construct
and a picture of the world
that around me moves
and death as an owl that watches
for our gates to yield
and the night to swallow whole
and what dispels to withdraw
and the bright mentality to succumb

if the sky is indeed anthropic
then life is to us a property
which we ought to defend
the curtains that once were wrent
from top to bottom
and the cap stones
that burst outwards

A VIEW FROM 300 METERS

for the world has shown its hand
and what secret concealed up its sleeve
its heart of darkness has been discovered
and unpackaged from its closets keep
and the morning was as by the rivers edge
when the clouds have parted
to the approach of dawn

with particulates of dew
impregnating the low land
steeping the break of day
as climbing up and out of the blackness
which entombs the caves beneath
we have put off this die that was cast
and we have found our pulse
and have entered into the fortified hold
even wolves had followed from a distance
because elsewhere there is no light

though the woods still
clothed in evening shadows
and darkest ink still clings
to the cold edges

we have found our pulse
and entered the fortified hold
that the day may entangle the moors
and press against the grim volumes
which fill as a cloud this broken land

for we have fainted before the murderers
and answered the alarm with vacancy
in the wind, the waste and the war

but our light can still vanquish
the unbelievable disarray
and the dismal collapse
can be swept to the fires

for the sun has climbed
high into the spring sky
and has sent its astir
and noble language
to again discern the aspects
which we have forgotten

for its rectification is a furnace
and its standard is a forge
so we have crossed over
hebron we have crossed
for so great a reminder

CONTEND

for the land should bare such an offense
the outrage and the abhorrence
the antagonism of death as death it self
come to vandalize and ravage
as if damage might overflow
the world we know
overthrown and undone
what odium of aversion
has parted our assurance
and broken our assets
how in a day has this malice
fanned against us a fire
and stirred at our wooden defenses
a smoldering flame
it has dug at our garrisons from beneath
and made fuel of our stockade
turning our keep into a pyre
and our familiar into tinder

our store has failed
we have discovered no response
to stay the rupture
or bar the breach
for we have become unseamed
we have become like a garment
which has rotted in the wet earth
blight has caught us in its scourge
for this sorrow has sheared off our fortunes
and polluted our endeavors

how we are exiled
at a distance we watch our cities burn
grim ambassadors wonder from the fires

I can hardly except what I see
when what I see is havoc
dissolving our accord
and pining all our hard fought synthesis
how can I survive
when we are so outnumbered
so we have become like castaways
hollowed and made of straw
if there is any recovery
or means by which to contend
it might be found
in aiming for the head

A SAILORS LAST ENTRY

for ropes it would seem
have descended from above
and stretched across the tameless land
reaching into every quarter
invading all our boarders
fording our blockade
only to, as some ghost that passes through walls
penetrate the earths living skin
probing the doors that lay beneath
to grab and pull
the world from the inside out

black flags it would seem
have been drawn up on polls
to snap and whip in the billowing
as winter branches in the moon light
cast shadows across our inner walls
reaching with fingers to touch our hearts hold
will they draw off our vestige and breath
turning our voice inwards
back upon our tung

and the sound of the sky
scraping against the earth
dragging us through the cannon field
leaving us exposed on the open hills
for in this place and in this time
I would look to you for I have nothing else
and I will hope from you an answer
because I have no answer
and I will speak to you my memory
for in memory I have a picture
and in my heart there is a mantle

but as a witness to a car wreck
seeing them cover the bodies with plastic
have I become a passenger
as the world rolls in toil
and the world rolls in woe
when sparks so small
have sacked the forests keep
and caused the great woods to fall
and caused the great woods brake
the sound of this sorrow would roar
when the south winds spin
and the force of this complaint would billow
as is the rush, the blast, the noise

do the hills beneath me move
while the life I knew
is thrown to the wolves
and do the hills beneath me flow
for on the horizon and at that place
where the earth and sky merge
one would suppose that all the seas
have beyond reason
transcended their bowl and basin
and filled the sky with its volume
and weighted the sky in its heap
as the walls of the abyss might reach
and stand up as in a dream
and walk as if a dreamer walked
and cover the earth with its deep
and fill the earth in its load
for black as black its self
has turned to us its face
and has looked upon us with its terror
for it would seem
the deepest durth and darkest part

of the oceans floor
has crawled from its silt bed
to take flight with wings that look like waves
and put on the body of a storm
and in turn take the form of a gale
and bare down on our coasts like walls that fall
like when the forest is full of flames
the furnace, the storm, the smoke

for skeletons it would seem
have interupted our once certain cheer
and have filled our streets with their bones
have the willows ceased
to weep because of the fear
have the willows stoped for the alarm
for hands have reached upon us
and gathered us from our storage
brought us forth from our package
and lift us out of our casements
to pull us from our wrappings
to take us from our place
for if the world it self were but
the contents of a dusty basement
creaking is what we have heard
as foot steps on the stairs descend

THE MEASURE OF CHARACTER

the dark would fly
as a wide and unfolding front
whose face was water
the color of coal
cool as a hole
indiscriminate
as disease her self
for with wroth and billowing blight
would cry a fearful complaint
steeped in wild overgrowth
bursting at the seems
grinding at our marrows bones
to find in us what will remain

what fraction of our hearts warm home
can divide into a similar feral repose
when men act in desperation
to discover the ice that in us might flow

for we were born but men
framed in upright form
anthropic constellation
who has with words shaped
a space for eyes to see
and a world to be
turning within our cares
our swaddled earthly garments
and the stars that we have named
with the weight of water as a standard

and it was upon this hill of our collective
and at the gate of our bodies keep
came as spiders spilling from their nest

as a smell that might gather
when the swamps mud rots in the summer sun
and the amphibians
lay stinking in the lengthening noon
so was the breach with which it broke
and pressed out over a season
undoing and dividing and breaking
pining as though force had joined with disdain
and together set fire to our wooden hold

VANDALS AT THE GATES

should a force as a mastodon
animate a paralyzed and vacant figure
as though the dissolution
of form destroying water
should breach the divide
and become a thing other than its natural estate
so should worms become men
should the crushed abyss become a virus
and spread its tentacles
through our urban domains
can we run to the hills
and escape the inundation

for an inhuman and alien tide
has crawled from its formless abandon
it has sown for it self members
gathered to it self bodies
it is loaded into vessels
and has discovered the sent of our mortal heat
so we think it has tasted the air
and discerned from its black abysmal fathoms
that the world of men lay beyond the waves

though the gulf was great
and its passage nonexistent
yet by the strange and inexplicable
as though the absurd were plausible
the impassable were negotiable
so dismay and joyless fright
hath discovered a passage
into our ghosted schells
and exhumed its spectral mastodon
its adverse and jittering possession

for the cold and the frigid are its familiars
so to cold remains it sought refuge
to ascend the cool, dark earth
and to climb from the shadows

thus its figures now stagger amongst the fog
and wonder the damp moors
wearing a bone yard as a vesture
we carry katanas and dispatch it
back to the chasms locker

this method we prefer
as guns seems too common an end
by which to return the injury
as well the loud crack is impractical
it requires continual ammunition

the katana blades, on the other hand
are up close and lend their use
to a certain pleasure
where in revenge swings into focus
and the gulf is released
from the feigned, unnatural bridge
and the offense of trespass
is abolished with a sword
and we for a moment
embody the nobility of feudal japan

THE RITES OF SPRING

for the tortured bloom of spring
would force forth her splender and sweet manner
in between the silos of our dreaming grief
the day it seemed was forever gray and slated
in the invasion of death to our cherished fortunes
for grim and grinding hollowed hills
have rolled in clapping collapse
upon our troubled shoulders
so the sight of her fair youth
seemed unfamiliar and unexpected
the dew of her mornings wealth
was strange and serial
how is this inception
who is this phosphorus gem
laying waste to our dour gloom
those flowers of happy pride
breaking on the gate of
our four enclosed walls
we will yet make gladness
of our pining distress
the romance of the vehement
the certainty of resolute
in the furnace of derision
for the dead have in a crowd of sirens
broken forth from the ground
for where veins onces held hot blood
now worms of hunger have animated
the form of a man
a ragged marauder and vacant invader
come to vandalize our advances
and pour on our silver hope ash and plight
when at once I was enveloped in their incursion
the earth seemed turned inside our

with roots reaching into the air
and the black underbelly
and the cavernous abyss
climbing into our grand sky
those arms seemed snakes
those mouths seemed as caves of the underworld
taking down upon its self
with wild disdain of its envious rot
how it might breath in
when it has no breath
how it might take back
what is now forever lost
to dispatch its desperation
back to the shallows
so is the crack of gun fire
imploding their envy
take them down to the shipyard after sun set
and cast their ruin back the foaming waves
for the locker will again receive their volumes

THE END OF DREAMS

if the iron sky should bend
and swing downwards in the storm
displacing the clouds
in the great bluff of atmosphere
so the hills would seem to swim
and the magnetic shields above
would resonate as some subsonic bell
and the coal night sky would glow green
and the world bellow would turn over
in its haunted mortal slumber

how have the stars piled with the weight of snow
baring down on our creeking roofs
and as though originating from the inside
the crack of midnight comes with a billowing
and the rolling hills that brake
upon our doors with the arms of the sea
a green and emerald sea
whose compressed oily black basement
turns from the inside out
and spills forth with arrows
that break our hearts solemn hold
and turn our cheer into a whirl wind
and our company into a fray

for what resort if any
may still afford our safety
and what hold our advocacy
for the icy bows of the abyss
have with watery arms
passed beneath our doors
and forded our gates
so with startled fright

we ran out under the night sky
to see what we would not have imagined
nor could it have entered into our thoughts
that the sky could above us fall

THE DIVISION OF DAY AND EVENING

the driving rain that billows
the whirling rain that blows
for all the wet and icy bows
and the longest pale night
in which the earth is but a passenger
awash and brimming
in the bluster that has taken hold
and turned us upside down
and shaken out of us
our fortunes
and our homes
and our health
and dispatched to us this message
the commonness of cruelty
and the wantonness of desperation
a despair that affords no sympathy
like a thief that cares not what he breaks

we turn on this clamor
as a door that opens
and our vision is not always
in what we see
so what looms over our moored vestige
the apple of your eyes
would turn as the turning of the day
and the night would climb
and ascend the hill
the alarm of your silent host
and the spire of those sated volumes

so also the vault of thoughts
that reflect not only the subject
grew more like the object of the day
and the absolute gesture of your heart
which I could not wish to restrain
though the world would seem to waver
and my heart would seem to sour
though the dour and crud ambling
of the crowd that sojourn at the poisoned well
and the vultures that circle

so also the city laments with their noise
so it would seem that an army of ravens
bolstered by the shadows
and the dark foil of disbelieve
might descend with ruin
their war and smoke and trouble

so was the work of our hands
blown to its very wits
and so was our mountain of grief
for the lame have spread
the wings of their conspiracy
and have breached the fortress of our fields
casting our crops into the fire

so I would breathe in the wet summer air
and the taste of the day
was not without abstraction
so I might dwell in the words that tell
that hold and keep of our beginnings

THE SICKNESS

what began as a fever
became then a plague
and in turn some other thing
a thing you would not have thought to be

that the dead would animate
with the reason of worms
and the voice of a grave intruder
and spread willfully
as though it belonged
to the whirling world
that always is passing
through the cool, crisp night
an envoy that declares
the passing of well being
from the rare and unusual
place that the living hold

our betrothal has become a thing of envy
when desolation should fan out on the wind
the flowers of romance have seemed
a mortal and solemn tower
as the eminent gray of the sea
and the walls of water that spike the sky
riding the warm drafts
that bridge the gap
and enrich the breadth of the motion
so should our heart
remain a stone amidst the storm

for the cruelest, unsympathetic animal
is not like to this disease
as it digs up in mens dead frame

the worst of man to be brought to bare
in one brawling marauder
of menace and mien spite
what disfigured mechanism of sickness is there
that should uncover this misfortune
this gross axiom of damage
that the vile may reflect its king
this baron of worms
and lodge of decay

for the swelling morning twilight
can not push back their obscurity
their black haunted ravine
that never unfolds into the open plain
nor manages to ford the ridge

some say the plague will pass
some push back the vandals

UNNATURAL PASSAGE

has autumn passed in an instant
has the icy holds of winter found us
in sudden and unnatural force
did the dead mans bones dry too soon
leaving not enough space for its animated form
to depart to God who gave it

for the dead are not at peace
and a curse upon them churns
as waves at sea that gather strength
driven in the angular wind and rain
for all our foliage and guarded green home
has in the space of an hour
turned to lye
the color of the sky a stone
the color of us a bone

there is no winter snow
to silence the air
no calm and bright morning
for as though in times past
when men fanned out on the earth
by means of wars cold conquest
so now maggots made of mens sinuses and limbs
have gathered at our walls
and this with out warning
as we thought this could not be
and in this way they fell upon us as fear
and fear it self hath taken up shield and spear
and upon us struck with unnatural force

who has stolen our autumn solace
and normal passage

have aliens stood upon the tops of trees
and pour blood down instead of autumn leaves
their skulls are swollen in inhuman fever
what alien star has penetrated their eyes
so they see the earth in nameless abandon
and our sun to them an alien orb
and our light an alien light
our homes only a creatures nest
that they will undo
for to us the stars are falling
and our steady and stable trust
know now only a sudden winter wale
only a disparing winters woe

our homes are haunted
the memory of us is fading
reducing down into
the disorganization of information
and the story of us grows dim
the dead amongst us roam

UNATURAL PASSAGE PART 2

if these wounds would speak
what an unfolding furrow
would seem to swallow all the world
whole as the sea
when ships sink beneath the waves
so our wounded city rolls
as the waves brake over her deck
and water, cold and indifferent
fills our hidden holds
and inundates with the force of dilution
pulling into pieces all our order
and undoing our plans

for such deluge will unpackage
and dismember where our feet stand
for the dead have become a torrent
and the vile have become our undoing
as upon the exits we will flee
and run from their sudden terror
for what madness is this
when the dead walk the earth
and the living live as mad men
for what sense can be made of ruin
such was our well-born sky lines
our noble tack and stately air
now our metropolis burns
and is washed in smoke
a thick and mudded smoke
that touches every thing
and pastes the air
with the smell of our grief
disease untamed has spoiled our hope
and nature herself has turned unnatural

as the waves brake over her deck
so as men adrift watch the sea consume
and see their mast and rigging slip beneath
so we turn our backs
on what was once civilization
because it is no more

THE MONTH IT IS... IS... FORGOTTEN

in the tall and sod wet grass
whose husk stood just above our brow
and in the spreading silence of dusk
the air so slightly moved
and the grass so slightly billowed
in the most hushed whisper
which can be imagined
slowly turning over
as though sound and light
had mixed in the ethereal oil of air
for the lulled face of earth
had in one passing moment
in one arching span seemed to breathe
or inhale us into its verdant constitution
our names move in and out of the shadows
as the grass exhales
there is a sent
of men full of venom
riding on the skull
to which worms have made
mince meat of the civil
a smoldering of gall
and as soon as the taste of the morose
had licked the humid air
as quick in the instant it was gone
but those residuals linger
we know of what plight they speak
maybe 50 meters to the north
where the woods loom
in crisp and certain vertical forms
where the wind passes over
and the tree tops sway
in a hushed voice

which if it spoke
might mention the wondering aliens of gray pitch
who in earth pined rags
must wonder on the borders
of our dominion

down in the grass
we stand on the ends of our feet
and stand and try to see
what is beyond the inundated marsh
but it is enough that we know
and we can tell
what our eye don't see
a world in eclipse
the air again softly breathes

THE INSTITUTION OF REST

my dreams of recent night
are neon crimson bright
if green could burn
if yellow could churn
could stir the world
into the red flush of sun set
across the globe at once
one great stretch of sky
as when the hills of grass are burning
and the mess of combustible earth
did together ignite
blanketing the day
in ash and orange light

and as dreams do
in a moment I was then running
breathing in the humid morning air
fleeing through the trees
figures of the nihilism
flank my retreat
until a mirror in the woods
swings into view
and into it I run
as though for a moment
I touched not the ground

this has become a door
to a memory
of a time before
when the world was young
and we were younger
before the plague
before the dead walked the earth

yet the mirror is not glass
but it if fabric
and as I breach its surface
the forest is torn
and the leaves fall
and the verdure and the azure
and the cool and wet smoke
that follows the creek
is undone from its roots
and separated from its saturation
and behind me the crows take flight
and I realize that the villains
are not yet far removed
and when, I hope,
will the world turn upside down
and shake the antagonists
from its shores

THE ROAD TO NO WHERE

with lament in hand our world has bent
and turned over in certain despair
for the clouds and storm have not parted
and the icy season continues across
all that we can see
for what purpose if purpose can be attributed
or to what end if an end will come
for with wide and smoking sorrow
has the better part of human nature
been thrust into the flames
as some cold and impartial black smith
hammering out of us the dross
and chasing to our very ends
the limits of what can be endured
for we are bent over the anvil
and the hot hammer breaks loose
what can be broken
and burns away
what can be burned

what is this giant wave of deep seas
that has inundated
that has washed over
in weight unbearable
has over turned
and uplifted
and taken apart our foundations
in one disseminating moment

as our blood began to flow
it would not be stayed
and as our hearts began to pound
there would be no release

and the earth seems not to cease
in its betrayal against us
for the dead which once slept
in its organic chambers
have over turned their crypt
and come looking into a world
that no longer is theirs

for decay which once spread inwards
as the dead return to the dust
now spreads outwards
and draws the living to their ends
how is this our cherished earth
turned on its side
to spill us from its swaddled crib
has she rejected her own
and forgotten her very sons

what frozen heart is this
that the world is changed
and her cities are shaken from their hold
and her capitals are discarded to the heap

we have run from the rush
and we have ran from the riot
and we have fled from the noise
and at the cliff we are stopped
for there is no where to run
and there is no where to flee
from this shaken globe
and this trembling planet
as inversion has invaded
and turned inside out
and has left bitterness and gal
at our door step

what is is left to us
we must wonder
and we must question
who are we to be
when what we were
is no more
when our world
has chosen for us death
and not life

THE ECLIPSE

the earth always casts her shadow
in the colossal sky
her azure magnetism
colors the edges in carbon blue
from the night we gaze into her shadow
as it sweeps the stoic stars
the timeless abode
of the great ceilings
seems to reach down through the gap above
and for a moment closes the distance

here the chaos burns
and the fear is broken
so the torrents will not always blast
and the world will not always last

as was an evening as this
when the night clouds parted
and the nocturnal hawks paused
and the terrestrial shadow
touched at first the sliver of the moon
then forded her silver bowl
and chard her skin in amber

does the moon there bleed
and morn her lamenting sister
whom rolls in toil
her burning capitals
that pass through the night
for the hills are doused in smoke
and have spiked the long valleys
with the smell of cracked walnut
making the atmosphere heavy

we now mark the lunar order
as the roman calender seems no more to apply
so also we think the time of the dead
can not always remain

STREETS THAT CROSS NO MORE BOARDERS

I see the trees pass
just outside the open window
I sleep a few hours
and then I'm up
it is hard to rest
when the dead stand in a shamble
carrying their grave on their sleeve
they walk but do not breathe
they look but do not see

this has become for me a nightmare
that only sleep relieves
for a moment
and then the world again
is wailing on the wind
and the sun returns not
after the storm
because all is alarm
when the dead are no more covered

some say it is a plague
some say a curse
some say nothing is real
some think this is the end
what can one make
of this waking dream
this unknowable fog
that clouds my eyes
does the world still roll to the east
or has the globe spilled its form
has the sea uncovered her legion

and disclosed her locker beneath
has the world become a thicket
a wide and haunted breach

will the road, I think
take me beyond this derision
I hold my hand out the car window
the pressure of air in my palm
seems to engulf
so that it is for a moment all I know
this road is on loan
I borrow its solace while I can
I wonder is this mine to have
this great and wide abandon
this yawning and scopic scene
it seems to enfold for me
to turn over beneath me
as though it has
no one else to know
no one else to see
what yet might become
so I have become its observer
its remnant citizen

I see the trees pass
just outside the open window
the woods are waving
at the sound of my passage
this combustion engine consumes the streets
this road takes me through to towns
that now litter the earth
as a discarded collection
of that which has lost its use
so the wind will take it
the seasons will reduce it

and the land will take back what it will

the windshield frames what will be
a bleeding heart was never enough
could not propel me fast enough
into where and when
and where before me the road bends
I shattered the back window with a brick
so that the wind would blow through

THE 10 MONTH WINTER

beneath the ash and pining dolor
beneath the dismal and dire rain
strongholds we have forged in charged earth
though the heavy hills are rolling
and the bright morning air again dissipates
because the haunted holds are smoking
filling the hollows in creeping cataclysm

for the ash
the cold
the southern sun

against this cheerless alarm we have built a wall
and against this downcast semblance
we have dug our trench
and set our corner stones
for the desire of the world it would seem
is to implode and collapse
to fail under the pressure
and to lay down for all is ravage

but we have taken heart
though the world is crashed
for the annihilated and decomposed
have overrun all quarter
and though it is so
and yet the world swims in destitution
the woe and exhaustion
is a cup we have thrown to the floor
for it had begun to bleed us
and it had begun to drain us
and as the color had fled our faces
and as the light dimmed in our eyes

some of us refused
and we heeded their call

we would not so easily be dispatched
and the waters around us parted
as a stone in a stream
and the almond tree put forth her bloom
though the winter still bound our gates
and the spring seemed yet impossible

for the ash
the cold
the southern sun

though we know we are years deep
in this blast of extinction that has subverted
and abolished our dominion in a day
and though the wind blows sparks
into our parched forests and dry fields
and the fires leap and the flames are not stayed
we will yet preserve
and we will still defend
because our spirit is not a material thing
and God has given rectitude

though the ash
the cold
the southern sun

God has given rectitude

THE PALE HARVEST

when the day passed beyond the hills in the west
and the uniformity of the dark
eased into its formal repose
the un-kept fields that wax in canker
as there is no one left to attend
so the over ripe crops are left to the crows
and the crows have none to inhibit
this their new dominion
with similitude the ravens lay claim
to the oaks and principle trees
and have breached the barns and silos
how many years I have forgotten to count
but not as many as one might imagine
yet it had been enough of a window
that, through, the black birds
have multiplied immeasurably
for they have attended our wake in numbers
and overflowed our memorials
as though by black flags
they have blanketed what of us that remained
for our ruins have been inundated
by birds of plunder
and so they stand watch over what was once ours
and they stand watch over the twilight
and carpet the land in their black vestige
their soot capes and obsidian cowls
as though the night it self had arrived early
and the day could not soon enough depart

some times we would watch from the tree lines
as the clusters of endless fowl
would churn at dusk
like bats returning to their lair

they would come to stay
upon the abased remnant
for it had become their province
and this their commonwealth
as for man, from this his quarter,
his claim to it is no more

to this spectacle we can but watch
as the inclining day slopes into crimson
couching the onyx armadas
in fathoms of flushed rouge
together falling into the arms of night

we were here not to glean the fields
because the chaff and grain
besides being devoured by the birds
was now rotten in the stocks
rather we were there for the mob
and the amorphous mass
of black winged messengers
for the volume seemed beyond nature
and the numbers were incredible to see
it was, we knew, the windfall of plunder
that garnered their explosion
it was yet eerie and unsettling
that the great fortune of this legion of birds
was on the wake and wet surge of our own forfeit
for the unhappiness of all our ill confluence
and the host of our expiration
could not be more observed
then by the unnatural multitudes
of crows and ravens
to venerate or rather taunt our ghastly exit

for so unnatural in turn was our damage

and so aberrant was our crash
for what furnace of grief could match
or what cataclysm could be like ours
or what antagonism is as this offender
that with worms for teeth and ruin for hands
has this marauder of offense come waring
to raise against us flocks of bane fiends
that look as men but are not
for damage has become a crown
and waste a wondering parade
for these worms and these maggots
have inundated our humanity
and torn at our bowls

for then while the show was over
and the evening watch was well at pace
so we our selves became perceptive of the dark
as we need to adapt and we must abolish
and we must become some one else
against this countless mod of libertine
this alien throng

for in them death has become a tyrant
and we have become as wolves
decay has become an assailant
and we have its ruin
it is as though the night they inhabit is thick
dark as dark is gloom
for night with us is as when the moon is full
for them a chandelier of caliginous dim
a rayless, opaque, lurid room
amongst the open night they wonder
we avoid their loss with reckoned motion
if they follow, we lead them to their end

A WINTERS TALE

the end of the world is weightless
pulled up from its roots
it has drawn near
baring its arms of cold and wind
the clouds waxed cinder
calling to the spraying seas
to feed its cumulus columns
and fill its holds

from dark labored skies
the snows began to fall
grinding stillness in a mortar bowl
and pulling together the rift and graft
as a thread draws twain fabrics together
in this way the colossus reared in motion
cool as the sea and dark as the ocean
as when vast masses of atmosphere
wrestle and roll in the body air
sending claps of resonance roaring
folding outwards as circles in water propagate
filling the world of men with cracks
so the world in discord rent
as a vessel adrift from its mooring

I am suspended
gazing upon the wide rift
the azure and silver earthen furrow
from which climbs the fog to join the clouds
the snowfall that continues
will last long through the night
a swaddled crib in which is contained
the soft billowing and hushed wail
the silent and still squall

from this we have sourced a feeling
frosted in chromatic night
light as the stars
are shimmering ghostly bright

today I see the earth has tilted
and the sky has turned to powder
the day has shed nights banal dark
clad instead with pale silver
having relinquished its lurid harbor

for we have been drawn up in these chords
and the clock has counted down these late hours
for the world has laid in dole and cinder
while a long cold night
has gathered from the north

all our loss has become blanketed
in a quiet winters tale
whose melody and cadence
might ford this bewildered chasm
for the river has become a surge
and its banks are marred in violence
so nature has flung us head long
in the epistemology in which we are hung

despite the language
by which we have contained our selves
as some sort of bereaved prisoners
yet you are still determined
to wrap our certain sorrow
and stretch our faint and boiled hope
out over the length and over the breadth
and push back the battle
and vanquish the pale and pining creature

and put off the bane havoc
that has assaulted all
to which we once belonged

for to this end
waxed in the winters white
spiked in azure bright
a table before us prepared
what we would endure
for the subverting extinction
would slay and disrupt
and so our unions did rupture
some would run while others hide
it mattered not when the waves broke
winter would come as an armada upon the seas
the snow would cover us in its sleep

THE END OF A WORLD

the sound arose as from a distance
slowing developing as from fragments
its members becoming
a certain force that sweeps upon miles
across land, across sea
if I could turn from it as the deaf
if I could look as though blind
and if I could not know
but that the world that I now know
and the life that I now hold
has been spiked in poison
in the sound of our abrogation

I can not say that I am looking forward
and I can not say that I expect a sign
to restore the desires I once perused
to train my thoughts again on that parade
for what ice age is this that has risen
from this inundation
did the world bleed water from the sky
then shed its warmth and comfort
how has the horizon frozen solid as a stone
and what is this to know
when knowing is ruptured
and what is this to see when seeing is fractured
and what is it to hear when the world is spinning
to forget did I lay my head on the open wind
swirling down in the storm of hail and rain

if we could make of this a war
we might gather our weapons
and we might gather our young men
and we would rise up on the face of the earth

and fall on this our adversary with all our fire
and all our armor and all our anger
and we would brake its hold on us
its camp against us would burn
and its plans which it has drawn against us
would fail
and we would overcome

but there is no war against this alarm
there is no battle against this villain
its forces are without shape
that our cross hairs may upon it fix
it is not a man that we might contend
it has brought against us our own fallen
it has roused against us our own dead
and it has made madness of reason
and for it we have no explanation
there seems no judgment
that can against this thing be leveled
for the plague of death is darkest business
and ruin is a grim complaint

what is left to us but
courage, and what is this our faith
for in us is yet resolution
that has drawn up in us a plan
to salt us in a forge
and in a furnace of the earth
to form in us a new thing
that has no resemblance
to who we once were
for we all began as someone else

for the men we were is perishing
and the future which we once thought

has come to an end
and if there is yet hope that remains
it may yet avail that we can begin again

thus this night we consort together
and have concluded what will resolve
and though it should cost us everything
when everything must go
and I understand now that I can not hold
to a world that is no more
because it never was going to last
and it was never going to stay
so we took it down the docks
while some light still lingered in the west
and the stars expanded in full view
and the east retreated to its circuit
so we put down the cannibal
and relinquished its body to the deep

DYSTOPIA

we are the living
cutting the world in twain
for the thicket is dense
the cheerless fabric has set
the world in whirling woe
the dark that lay bellow
has climbed the columns of the earth
and built against us a burning
to smoke us from our bastion
and spoil our long held home

so we have put on the rampart
and cloaked our state in bulwarks
for we have become a garrison
and bound our selves as a troop
to divide the cankered scourge
though our gentility has waxed coarse
and our polished chrome megaliths
are marred and shattered
for fires have despoiled
and the blowing storms have dissolved

our urban courts are overgrown
our ground floor windows broken
curtains whip in the bluster
our roof tops succumb to the winter
now we are a shadow
we are the troops that ford the river
our galaxy above us shimmers
with the circuits of the night